SOULBOUND -1
It Can't Be Him

by

AK Bhardwaj

SoulBound -1
It Can't Be Him
by AK Bhardwaj

ISBN: 978-93-67142-31-8

Published by

DOUBLE 9 BOOKS
2/13-B, Ansari Road
Daryaganj, New Delhi – 110002
info@double9books.com
www.double9books.com
Tel. 011-40042856

ABOUT THE AUTHOR

Aditya, known by his pen name AK Bhardwaj, is a 15-year-old literary prodigy who has quickly made a name for himself in the world of fantasy fiction. With a natural talent for weaving complex narratives and building immersive worlds, Aditya's debut novel is a testament to his creativity and dedication. His writing captures the imagination, transporting readers to a universe filled with epic battles, intricate power dynamics, and unforgettable characters. Aditya's journey as an author began at a young age, fueled by his love for stories that push the boundaries of reality. His ability to create multi-layered plots and deeply relatable characters has earned him praise from both peers and mentors. Despite his youth, Aditya writes with a maturity and depth that belies his age, drawing readers into the rich tapestries of his tales. Currently, Aditya is passionately working on the second part of his novel, aiming to delve even deeper into the intricate world he has created. His drive to continuously improve and expand his storytelling shows a commitment to his craft that is truly inspiring. As he continues to hone his skills, Aditya is set to become a significant voice in the realm of fantasy literature, with many more stories to tell and worlds to explore.

CONTENTS

TO SHAWSHANK BHARDWAJ

ACKNOWLEDGMENTS

All the things happening in my mind are on screen or paper. I have spent days and nights making this thing considered a masterpiece. But still, it is just a normal dark fantasy novel. Still, I consider this a masterpiece because it is the finest piece of art I have ever made.

I have written 3 novels but have yet to make plans to publish one. I am just a normal boy dreaming of becoming the greatest author in the world. I want to express my gratitude towards my parents, friends, and brothers. Specifically Shawshank Bhardwaj (one of my elder brothers) for providing me direction through honest and valuable feedback. His feedback gave me a summary of my areas of improvement.

I wrote this novel using only a notebook, laptop, and artistic mind. I am also thankful to them.

Chapter 1
Bloodbound village

Darkness has spread worldwide but some light is making some space in it. The light is coming out like a laser from the show of the year in Khandar. Vikram Agnivesh holds this show every year. He is the village chief of Khandar. Everyone has a stereotype of a village chief, every one of them is short, selfish, and owner of a big belly and money a normal villager can never think of. Vikram passes all of them except owning a big and fatty belly. He has a very lean body.

"It's the best lighting I have ever seen," One man said with an open mouth. The lighting is fascinating. All the villagers glanced at the show's decoration and somehow felt blessed. All just appreciate the beauty of red and white tents and some cushioned sofas with a strange yet heartwarming smell.

They all took their seats on the sofa. There are enough sofas that everyone can sit there comfortably.

"I wonder what Vikram will declare today," a woman said to her husband. The crowd creates cacophony in the atmosphere. " May I have your attention please?" said one deep and strong voice. Vikram starts to give a speech " Till now we have made our village well-developed enough that we are now living in a very peaceful village" Everyone praises his words with their claps. " Today on my birthday," he continues " I have some important information and a lovely message for you all. From the day after tomorrow, we have decided on a policy named 'Nishulk shiksha yojana'. No matter where they belong, every child will get a free education in government school. The whole purpose of this Yojana is to give quality education free of cost. One more thing, we will give our proper attention to our village culture and tradition," . He declared about 18 new things that can help in the development of the village. When he is about to end the speech, he leaves a message for all the citizens. " All I have achieved so far in my life is not greater than your love. Your support has made me the head of this village. Pals, we have so many ebbs and flows in the village but by your kind support and love, we are not prone to that much. I want to express my gratitude toward you all and my security team. thank you" . The audience responded with a huge round of applause.

The cake has been cut, and the villagers will now enjoy a delicious and lovely meal.

"What's that sound?" a man said to his friend. Voice has turned into an echo of the show. The sound is like an animal scream when hungry, but it is a little sharp, and villagers guess it is of a child crying angrily. " Maa, I am not getting a good feeling," a terrified child said to his mother. Everyone starts to give their attention to the forest the voice came from.

They all are just trying their 100% of Thinking what it can be. Some of them say that this is an animal. Some say it's a lost kid from his tribe in the woods.

The sound has become like a horse patting on the ground when it runs but it is like a human is running like a horse.

Suddenly lightning strikes the woods and all the trees start to burn up. Everyone gets terrified and decides to run but it's too late. Villagers begin to depart from the event. Only half of the population has passed the gate and the security guard closes the gate. " Try to understand we can't open the gate right now. We should focus on our life first" Vikram said.

The sound echoes again but it's pretty close. The sound is coming from outside the gate. It's like that entity is just lurking in front of the gate.

"Please stay behind, you are risking your life," one security guard said " I can understand that your family members are outside" .

They heard screams from outside and they could surely tell that it was their family members seeing death in front of them. " My husband! I am going to kill it and eat it alive" a woman cries.

After a long period of dark time where all the villagers are diving into their loved one memory, the screams are finally stopped. The chaos has come to an end. The security guard opens the gate. The villagers rushed out crying. Vikram also ran out and saw a bunch of dead bodies lying. The soil of the ground has absorbed all the blood in it. All bodies seem to be seriously wounded but there is one body that has no wounds but splashes of blood around his body. The body is of a toddler wearing a school shirt and black trousers. his teeth have turned red. It seems like he has drunk blood.

***

"Wow Baba, so intense and gripping story you have made," a boy of around 15 told his father. " It's not the story I have created, The supreme power creates it. It's a real-life incident in the village of Khandar. After this incident, Khandar was named 'the dark Khand'. Manan, the world you are seeing with your eyes is not the one you will experience in the future" his father said. " No way this can be real," said Manan.

Manan is a freezing boy with good physical genetics. If the one disrespects his culture and religion, he will not do much but beat the one so badly that he/she will not get up from bed for around 6-7 days. His strength automatically increases in a battle. He has good control over his hormones.

Manan wakes up from his peaceful night nap on a very charming day. His house is smaller than a palace. It has 2 bedrooms, a bathroom, kitchen, storage and a basement. The basement is like the room of his father. He lives with his father only. His father spends most of his time in the basement doing paranormal research.

"Baba!," screams Manan half asleep as he cannot find him in his house. He goes to the basement with the hope that his father is maybe doing research but no. He only finds a folded and crumpled page with the written 'open please'. The tension rises in his mind like a bright yet dark sun. Without wasting more time he unfolds the page. He is also unfolding the mystery with little and trembling hands.

Chapter 2
Meet your new friends

He unfolds the page and the mystery at the same time. The page turns into a letter. He checked the name and saw his father's name, Arjun Vidyvansh. Handwriting clearly states that it is written in a hurry. It is merely understandable. Ink is also spilt on the paper at the corner. He starts to read. the letter goes like this:

Dear Manan,

I know this is hard to digest but I will try to tell you in very short. I am Arjun, your father. Your grandfather and grandmother were lovely parents to me—one day wken I went to my maternal house with my parents in Khandar. On our way, we saw a man lying on the ground. My father goes to help him but the man turns out to be a demon. With his sharp fangs and nails, he pierces my parents in front of me. I was completely blank at that time. All I could think was to run and seek some help. I went to a police station but the police did not trust my words.

Years passed, and I became an adult. I was raised at an orphanage for free. I married a girl I loved in that orphanage. I got a job. We got blessed with a baby boy which are you but Your mother passed away as she gave you birth. Then I started paranormal research so that I could prove that demons exist and we have to be aware of them.

Now it's time to tell you a harsh truth. Manan, I will never come to our house and if I can survive, I will never ignore the opportunity to meet you. I have no idea if you are ready, but you will carry on my research from now on. I got you admitted to a government hostel for free food and skelter. Take all my research journals from drawer number 1 but do not open drawer number 2, you are not ready for it. I apologise for my act that you have to be alone at this age but it's only for your safety. If possible, please forgive your baba and remember that your baba will always love you and never let other memories get hidden in his head.

By

Arjun Vidyvansh'

He throws the letter. Letter, floating in the air, reaches his feet. He was so blank and hollow then that he wondered if it was a dream. A sudden and massive change in life is enough to traumatize anyone. Tears are escaping his eyes and falls to the ground. He is standing here silently like a statue, not moving at all. When his brain is done decoding and digesting this reality, he falls to the ground on his knees and screams. Trauma is so large that his body gives up and then he faints.

One day, he saw himself lying on the bed of the hospital. One man is sitting beside him. "So you get consciousness now. Let me introduce myself. My name is Sandeep. I am your Father's friend. I was. Your father has given me responsibility for you until your hostel session starts. For the next 1 month you will live with me" Sandeep said. Manan asks "Where is Baba?". Sandeep thinks and answers " No one knows. Hey, why are we here? We have to go now,"

Manan sits in the car and goes to Sandeep's house. The house is quite large. " Your father is very mysterious. He gave me one key and said to give it to you," Sandeep handed one rusty key to Manan " I have one more surprise for you. your dad's journal and a book about demonic shit" Then he handed Manan a bundle of 7-8 journals and one book with yellow crinkled pages. " he also gave me one training schedule, which is a little hectic, I wonder if you can follow it" . He puts his hand in his trouser's pocket and grabs one piece of paper with the training schedule " This training will improve your reflexes, strength, speed, and stamina, and helps you to forget all the shit happening in your life. In my opinion, you should forget all damn things of the past and just move on," he said.

Manan, listening to his words, doesn't let any expressions burst on his face. His personality is becoming more cold day by day. He grabs the page and starts to observe it. He took a great sigh of tension.

"OK, but who the hell are you to tell me all this crap," Manan said. Sandeep took a sigh and said, " Damn, you should also add one brain exercise. I have told you before that I was your father's friend, Sandeep" .

"I still have no idea what you are but if you are my father's friend, I will live with you and follow that training," Manan said. His blank face is not curable. His face becomes as deep as a sea that one can see but cannot understand what's hiding in it.

This 1 month passes like 10 years for Manan. He is doing his training without taking any breaks. That's why He has many cramps in his muscles. He can't sleep properly because of his father's memories riding in his mind, how he was used to telling him stories, how he was used to cooking his favourite food for him. Every night, tears escaped his eyes, and made his way right to his pillow and got soaked by it. Usually in normal conversation, he starts to cry because of his father's memory overflowing.

When his hostel session starts, Sandeep and Manan go to the hostel for all the admission work. When all the work is complete, Manan walks to Sandeep's car and picks up two bags. When he is going to enter his hostel, he sees Sandeep standing at the gate. " So, you are finally going. just take care of yourself. If you have any information just send a letter to the address on the back page of journal number 5. Goodbye, little champ" Sandeep said. Manan's blank face suddenly changes to a crying face. He hugs Sandeep very tightly. " Goodbye and thank you, we will surely meet again" he cries. He enters his hostel and makes his way to the 4th floor. He walks to pathways of the 4th floor and sees boys rushing toward him, looking into a book. They both strike very badly. " What the hell is wrong with your damn freaking eyes, boy," Manan said to the boy. " I am sorry," the boy said. " no issues," said Manan.

When Manan entered his room, he saw a boy sitting on a chair next to the window and looking out from the window. " Excuse me, That's my room," Manan said in a cold voice. " We are sharing this room," said the boy. His voice is more cold and depressed than Manan's. The boy finally turns to Manan and Manan sees his face for the first time.

His face is very dull and a little dark-toned with deep and stunned eyes with 2 dark circles. His body is looking a little down and weak.

"If that is so then hi I am your roommate Manan Vidyvansh," Manan said in a bright voice with a little smile. " Well, my name is Sehel Shayanka, nice to meet you," said Sehel.

Manan starts to set up his place. He got one bed, a side table, and a study table. He starts to unpack his bags.

Chapter3
Bully

He opens his first bag with a dull excitement. He extracts his clothes and then his academic books. Then he grabs his second bag, extracts some other clothes, and then Arjun's journal. when journals are in his hands, his face becomes dull. He bites his hand so that he can drink all of his pain. He puts down his journal and that demonic book. He grabs the keys given by Sandeep. " Hey," said the sleepy voice of Sehel " What's this?" . He pointed to journals. " Nothing great, you should not know that," said Manan " Tomorrow is our first day at the hostel. We have to go to bed early if we want to attend our school," Manan said with fake enthusiasm.

The next day, Manan wears his school uniform and goes to mess to get food in his belly. " Damn, my stomach is feeling like hell!" Manan said in a low voice so no one could listen. " Hi," Manan hears one voice from behind. The voice is of the boy who strikes Manan in the corridor. " I am very sorry for yesterday. I was in a hurry" said the boy. " Come on, you baby shit. That's not a big deal," said Manan. The boy has got red cheeks and a slim body. " My name is Advik, nice to meet you Mr. -Err," Advik said and offered his hand for a handshake. " Manan Vidyvansh, nice to meet you too," said Manan, accepting his handshake and friendship.

They all got settled at desks in the classroom and started to focus on lectures. In their free time, Manan notices one girl with a cute face staring at him. By getting all guts, he goes and asks " What's your name?" . The girl blushes and replies " Devika" .

"So, Devika, do you want to be my friend?" Manan said but he knew deep down that the thing he was doing was wrong for his life. With a pang of deep guilt burning inside, he leaves his classroom without her reply.

Advik watches everything and goes to look for Manan. He spots Manan in the washroom. He has covered his head with his hands like a blanket. " Hey," Advik said " What are you thinking? Anyways, I must say boy, you are just too serious and cold about your motives, intentions, or goals. The way you control your male hormone to explode over that cheap girl is amazing man"

Manan sees him and gives him a gentle smile, he appreciates his praises. " Thanks, buddy," Manan said.

They got out of the washroom. They saw kids departing from school to the hostel. " Oh, finally this boring shit got a freaking end," Manan said " Wait, I forgot my backpack." . When he reached the front of his class, he saw a bunch of boys surrounding Sehel thoroughly. " Hey, what's happening here?" Manan asks. He saw one guy holding Sehel's collar and threatening to give him some money. " Leave him alone, you freaks," Manan said, losing his temper. " What if we do not? What can you do to protect that skinny from us' ' The Guy who is holding his collar leaves Sehel and makes eye contact with Manan.

Out of the blue, he throws his punch at Manan. Very easily, he holds his fist and starts to squeeze it. All the guys standing there attack Manan but he dodges all of them. " My turn, let's play" Manan throws one punch at a guy's teeth. Some of the teeth fell off. He starts crying.

All of them start to run as fast as they can. " Thanks," Sehel said in a mild voice.

The awkward silence starts to rise between them. It breaks when Manan enters the classroom and takes up the bag. " Come on, it's time to go to our room and give some rest to our body," Manan said. He is constantly trying to move on and change his behaviour but inside, he is bleak and lonely. Still, he is trying to make some new friends.

"Finally, it's the time," Manan said on a very dark night. He is sitting on the chair with one of the journals in his hands. He turns the pages and reaches the page with the heading *' research 1 " Rakta'"* .He starts to read it very carefully.

'Rakta is one of the soul-bound demons in the world. It was mainly worshipped in Khandar village. It has been searching for a strong host for more than 100years. It comes to action when its host drinks human blood and deactivates when it wants. But with strong willpower and motivation, the host can get control over it.'It has much power. Some of them are weather manipulation, telekinesis, super strength, and many more. If anyone drinks the blood of Rakta's host body will start to control him. Rakta's host can only be a male human. For the past few years, Rakta has gone missing from the temple.'

"Hey, what's that," Said Sehel. He starts to read it from a distance. " It's interesting" . Manan spots him " Hey, you shouldn't be reading that." He says in an amazed voice " Fine, Sehel, I am a paranormal investigator and I have only one job, to find the origin of the demons and reap it off. I am not sure if you have heard the story of Dark Khand, currently, I am in search of one of 3 demons who made the village downtrodden. So, are you in?" He presented this offer with a handshake. " OK, still better than sitting and inspecting the past," Sehel jerked his hand very softly and accepted the offer.

Manan started to discuss his progress in the research. " I have decided to start with the Dark Khand. I have a full suspicion of Rakta because that boy has some blood in his mouth and also this journal says that Rakta was mainly worshipped in Khander." Manan said in an enthusiastic voice. " believe me Sehel, we will be contenders in this world but you have to dream it also"

By saying these words, Manan makes some effort to make Sahel's personality happier and more enthusiastic. They overpower their sleep for research.

The next day, while grooming for school they look at each other and nod softly. They have become aides for each other in the past few days.

"Today is a very vicious day, the sports teacher will select some students for a football match held at our school only," Advik said in a cheering voice, " I eagerly want to be the goalkeeper of our team." Enthusiasm is clearly shown in his voice. " Oh really," Manan said, " then, all the best. Teacher will surely perceive your talent, believe me" . " Thank you for motivating me," Advik said, shaking his hand.

***

"OK students, pay attention here. You all are 25 kids but I only need 11 to complete my team. Now I will distribute the team and I will observe and select some of you"

The Team was distributed, and Manan and Sehel are on the same team. Advik is on the other side, standing at the goalpost. The match begins, Manan is playing very well and Sehel is also cooperating with Manan. They have become an unbeatable duo. The first half has ended. Manan and Sehel walk together to their rest point but suddenly Sehel stops walking. " Hey, what's the matter- Oh! shit," Manan said quietly, seeing his blank eyes without pupils. Suddenly, Sehel fell forward and rested on his knees. His pupils come back. " Hey, what the hell is happening with you," Manan said. Sehel replies " Tell Advik to protect his nose. " Are you alright?" Manan asks, ignoring his advice. " Yes, I am good, it happens frequently," Sehel replies.

The second half began, and the match went very interesting. Both teams managed to push the match to the same point. Both teams scored 6-6. One boy from Manan's team got the ball and was going to shoot the ball in the goalpost but it was protected by Advik. Accidentally, he got hit by the ball on his nose and then his nose started bleeding.

He lies on the ground, and the crowd surrounds him. His mouth is wide open so some of the blood from his nose gets in his nose.

"Ah! Ah! I drank blood! Run away" Advik said mysteriously.

"Why is he telling us to- no, he can't be," Manan said in an agitated voice. He knows that Sehel has something. He approaches Sehel. " Hey, tell me honestly what did you see?" Manan asks in a hurry. Sehel grunts " Destruction"

Chapter 4
Advik

Everyone standing on the playground just ran away saving their life. But Manan and Sehel stayed there watching an enormous layer of smoke and a change in weather. they hear a loud warcry. Advik screams frustratedly. " I can say he is Rakta, Rakta has taken his body because of his low willpower. Sehel, we have to stop him as quickly as possible, he shouldn't cross the main gate. You should go and tell everyone to get locked up in a classroom. I think I have to fight him." Manan said to Sehel. Sehel can see the tension and blankness in his voice.

Advik rushes out from the smoke by using his hands like legs. He starts to run on his 4 legs towards Sehel. " Watch out, Sehel" Manan screams and jumps between them. The ground shatters and drinks the blood. Manan holds Rakta's jaw with both his hands bleeding. Manan faces Rakta in the battle. Rakta swings his hand with sharp nails. Nails got stabbed in his back. " Manan!" Sehel said in a loud voice. " Nails are just in the muscles. I'm going to be okay. You should go now." Manan said in a painful voice. " get off to me, freaking shit!" Manan said by pushing Rakta back with a strong kick.

"Advik, I know you are here. Please, use your willpower" Manan tries to embrace Advik. Rakta screams, but more loudly this time. " I don't think you are going to catch up, let me help you," Manan said in a low voice. He rushes and punches him in the shoulder. Rakta raged and attacked with his sharp pointed fangs and nails. Manan dodges them by getting some shots and gets stabbed in his body. Manan is covered with blood but still fighting with him. His whole energy got drained all he is capable of is just one punch. He tightened up his fist and ran towards Rakta. Rakta saw him with a punch. He screams and all the ground quakes and collapses. Manan got tossed by Rakta by his powers. Manan fell on the ground very hard. Manan got unconscious.

Rakta walks towards him and holds on to eat him But somehow he stops and starts to struggle with the mind. Advik is trying to defeat the inner monster.

After a while, Manan found himself in a dark space with no walls or anything. He tries to scream but fails. Words are trying to escape his throat. He hears a woman crying. He follows the voice and finds a lady holding a baby. She got terrified by seeing Manan and said " Please, don't hurt my baby, you can hurt anyone once my baby is in a safe place. please, I beg you." Then out of the blue, the Woman starts to spit blood and goes to her death along with her baby. Manan realizes that it is some kind of a dream. Suddenly, everything started to shake and explode. Manan Regains consciousness and opens his eyes. He is feeling rage and some increase in his physical abilities. When he looks at his arm, he dives into complete shock. he saw that his veins had turned black

Manan saw Rakta lying on the ground with a pain in his eyes. He is growling loudly. Suddenly, he gets up and punches Manan. Manan falls back but lands on his foot. Manan's rage gets overpowered and then he runs towards him. Rakta uses telekinesis but Manan has no effect. Manan punches the demon. The demon also starts to rage. After a while, Demon ended with a big fight of punches and kicks. He smiled at Manan. His smile looks like he is impressed by Manan.

Manan holds Rakta by his neck and starts to punch his face. Rakta roars and then the weather takes a turn. A thunderstorm starts to cover a clear sky. One thunder strikes down the ground and hits Manan. Manan again goes unconscious. His body becomes crisp and dark. " It can't be," Sehel said looking through the window. " Is he dead?"

Manan is not responding. Rakta is there watching everything. He smiles in amazement. Then he does something unexpected. He tears his skin out of his hand. That part of the skin was covered in the blood properly. Rakta opens Manan's mouth and forces him to chew it.

Manan in a half-sleep state chews everything. Rakta leaves Advik's body through his mouth in the form of smoke. The smoke enters Manan's body.

Manan finds himself again in the dark place But with a demon with all black hairs and wings like dragons with red eyes. It looks like a wolf. It has large fangs and nails. It ran to eat him with a wide open mouth. " I know who you are. I will not let you take over me. You are damn Rakta—the demon of Khander. My body is not yours" Manan speaks out loud. Rakta stops at his place and starts to scream. As time passed, he got converted into the sand. Manan goes and grabs the sand. He rubs the sand all over his face.

He gains consciousness after a few hours. He saw himself lying in his hostel room. He saw Sehel standing beside him. " Are you alright?" Sehel asked very softly. " Yeah, but where the heck are the others? Holy shit, where is Advik?" Manan asked in a dull voice. He jumps out of bed and starts to walk without knowing that he has been stabbed multiple times. His body is half covered with bandages. When he entered Advik's room, he saw many students standing beside his bed. He also saw some teachers standing there.

Everyone starts to stare at him absurdly. No one is paying attention to Manan, all are busy checking Advik.

Chapter 5
Cult

"Don't be upset dude, nobody cares about anyone," Sehel said to confront Manan. " Man, but I saved them, not him," Manan said in a shallow voice. Manan can feel the presence of a new entity in his body. " But it will be fun to see what Rakta can do," Manan said, " Advik hates me now, right?" He asks Sehel. " Kind of, he is saying you stole his weapon," Sehel answered. Manan takes a sigh, " After all, it's a life. we have to live it to nail it. No matter if they hate you like hell or love you like heaven." Manan smiled, " Ah yes, I want to ask you a question," . Sehel nodded his head. " how the hell can you predict the freaking future?" Manan asked. Sehel sips up the saliva in his mouth. " OK, this is because of my blood, Shayanka's blood. I have no idea how this works, I experienced it several times. I think I have this trait only," Sehel answered.

Manan shows some enthusiasm about the connection of inherited blood to demonic powers. " Man, I also experienced it while fighting Rakta. I saw some weird moments and gained some physical traits," Manan said. Sehel replies, " I think we should sleep now, it's midnight" Sehel points to the wall clock. " Good night"

***

Manan slept well and missed today's school. " Holy shit, I missed today's school," Manan said, rubbing his head with almost closed eyes. " Anyways, I got some time for investigation." He saw Sehel's empty bed.

He sits at his study table and opens up the same Rakta's journal. He turns the page and reads the heading *'Rakskas'* " Another one, go ahead," Manan said to motivate himself.

*' The strongest Soulbound, Rakskas, had been missing for more than 200 years. It is said that one evil demonic cult worships Rakskas's fluid. There is only one way to activate it, just take a sip of that fluid. Rumours are that the cult never wants to get revealed. It is situated in the woods. A boy with trauma can have this. Rakskas can transfer his abilities to other soulbound holders.'*As soon as Manan jumps to the next paragraph, He hears a knock on the door. He closes the journal and opens the door. Advik is standing there with open arms. He approaches

Manan and hugs him tightly with tears in his eyes. " Hey, What happened?" . He can't reply with that many tears. Manan Confronts him, places him on a chair, and lets him relax. After a while when the situation got normal, Manan started a conversation.

"Aren't you supposed to be at school at this time?" Manan asks. Advik replies in a weak voice " Doctor advised me to take one day rest. I am thankful to you, Manan," . " For what?" Manan said in a humorous tone. " For saving my life from that demon. It gives me nightmares every time and I see some places and other creepy demons, Sometimes of my father beating my mother with a belt," He sobs " He does not have the right to beat my mother, no matter if he was a head of the village," . Manan got tensed and asked " Village?" . " Yes, Khander," Advik replies in a crying voice. " Advik Please don't tell me your father is Vikram Agnivesh." . Manan said in a surprised voice. " How do you know?" Manan got a complete shock. He can relate all incidents of Khander. The cause of Dark Khand is sitting next to him.

"Your full name is Advik Agnivesh, right?" Manan asks. " Yes, what happened I just shared about my past a little bit," Advik replies. Manan's voice got low. " I need your help, Advik, Can you elaborate on your childhood a bit," . Manan grabs a notebook and a pen. Advik started " My childhood has been very rough. I can't remember everything but I have some glimpses of my childhood. I am very attached to my mother but not to my father. Often, he drinks alcohol, grabs the belt, and beats my mom. My mom was a weak woman. She never took her stand and fought that demon disguised as her husband. Only 1 time did she threaten him that she would speak about his dark side to the media. Vikram was so tense about it that one day, he grabbed the knife and stabbed it in my mother's throat. While she took her last breath, he called out my name loudly. When my mother died, I was very depressed because it was too much for a toddler aged 3. I have no idea why I am living, Vikram also mistreated me. He was just hungry for respect and power. He can touch any limit to get respect and he does. One day when I was sitting in my room wearing an old dusty school dress, my father came to my room with evil eyes. He grabs my hand and pulls me. I screamed and cried very hard but no one listened. I don't know how but I fainted. When I woke up I found myself in the middle of the forest. I could hear all the voices of enthusiasm from that show. I saw a bearded man holding 1 glass container full of blood.

Firstly, he apologized and then poured it into my mouth. Then the only thing I can remember is just blood and dead bodies" Advik concluded. Manan dived in complete shock. " Are you freaking serious? Is this a dream or something? What the hell!" Manan exclaimed. " I think you need some time for this. Ok, then we will meet tomorrow at school," Advik said in a confronting voice.

Manan grabs his journal and jots down everything with the heading *'Dark Khand'*. He starts to write everything Advik says. He writes for more than an hour. He dives into the flow state. He writes down every scenario.

Sehel returns from school and finds Manan sleeping at the table. He tries to wake him up from sleep but fails. Sehel sits on the bed and changes his clothes. Suddenly, when he is about to leave the room, Manan wakes up out of the blue, fainting and sweating. " I saw that, cult, I saw that. Sehel grab your shoes we are going into the woods"

Chapter 6
That masked guy

Manan and Sehel got ready by wearing a pair of sports shoes. " What happened? Can you explain?" Sehel said, " Also it's a shiny afternoon. We can't pass the main gate." Manan smiled and said " Main gate? Who is passing that" . Manan and Sehel leave their room with a lock.

They reach the backside of the hostel. They stand in front of a big wall hiding a dark forest behind it. Sehel notices a metal wire connected to the electric supply on the top of the wall. " We cannot touch this wire, first we have to do something about that electricity," Sehel said in a warning voice. " You are right but the security guard is sitting. We cannot go there and turn off the supply directly. we have to come up with a plan" .

A fat security guard with a big moustache sits idle with a newspaper. Manan and Advik go to the short-ground front of the guard's cabin. Manan punches one guy and starts to run " Hey freak, catch me if you can," Manan says while running. The kid starts to chase him. Manan stopped in front of another kid and said " This kid is trying to mess with you!" Manan said. The kid with a loaded punch chasing Manan is about to throw the punch but Manan dodges. They got hit directly by that other kid. " Hey, what's up with you man!" He says in anger and starts to fight.

Manan approaches the guard " Hey go check there is a matter in the small ground" . Guard went in a rush. Manan calls Sehel who is standing and waiting for Manan. Manan opens the door of the Electric supply and turns it off. " It was easy by the way. " Manan said humorously.

Sehel climbs up the wall followed by Manan. Both jumped down from the wall to the dusty and leafy ground. They look up and see a bunch of large trees. They can hear the sounds and screams of animals. Manan starts to walk deeply in the forest. Sehel also follows him. They saw different kinds of birds there.

"We should go now. There is nothing in here," Sehel said with low energy. Manan is going to reply to him but he sees something suspicious in the middle of the forest. He sees one lamp hanging on the branch of the tree by a rope. " What the hell is that?" Manan said in a confused voice. He goes forward in the direction of the lamp. He observed that the lamp was connected to something by strings. There are many of these bound with trees.

They follow the lead and find themselves in front of a wooden gate. Manan hesitates to touch the gate but Sehel normalises it. Sehel opens the gate. They both went inside and saw some weird masked guys doing some satanic ritual. Manan notices the Rakshas's fluid kept in an ancient glass bottle kept at the middle of the ritual. That cult is reciting some kind of spells and curses. Every cult member is busy with rituals. Manan and Sehel plan to steal the jar but they don't know how because the jar is surrounded by cult members. As soon as they can come up with the plan, the ritual ends. Every member notices them and three of them rush towards them with a long dagger in each hand. Manan pointed at a tree, trying to tell Sehel to hide there. Sehel runs towards the tree. One of the three guards jumps and swings the dagger to cut Manan's head. Manan kneeled, dodging the attack but when he saw another dagger approaching him. He jumps and dodges that attack too. He saw another dagger swinging towards him from the right. Manan holds the handle of the dagger and the hand of one of the guards and punches him in the stomach. But he feels his stomach get harder. Then he punches on his face and jumps back. He notices one thing: they are not attacking together. When Manan is fighting with a tough stomach, the remaining 2 can attack him but are standing idle. Manan, using this information, dodges the attacker's attack and goes for the remaining two. Manan punches them both with a powerful fist. But he didn't notice the dagger behind him. He tries to dodge it but tough stomach is successful in giving a little scar on Manan's throat. Tough Stomach goes to the remaining guards and grabs one more dagger. He recites some Mantras and then Daggers catch fire with some electricity around them. " Is it the right time to call out Rakta for help? No, but this weapon looks so deadly. I think it will be fun for Rakta too," Manan thinks in his mind " Hey, you Tough Stomach, bring your deadly weapon because it's time for some Rakta time,"

Manan rubs his thumb on his throat's cut and starts to suck it. Nothing happened. Manan was shocked " What!" . As soon as he can figure out the reason, he gets hit by the handle of the Dagger, thanks to his reflexes.

Manan falls so hard that the ground cracked. He cannot handle so much pain. He can't control his screams. He also can't control his consciousness. He fell unconscious and lay on the ground. The guard starts to approach Manan's body with that dagger to cut him down but he stops after getting close to Manan's body. His body is producing immense energy. After some time his body starts to produce a ruby red flame and that flame has surrounded his body.

His body teleported to the back of the guard. " Do not touch my young descendent. Fight me, coward," said Manan in a manly voice. After some seconds, Manan punched the guard with a punch covered with flames. " Shame on you, my single punch is more powerful than your both daggers," . Sehel, seeing all of those behind the tree, was shocked " What are you? Manan" Sehel said in a low voice.

Manan is fighting with the guard very hard without getting any pity. Suddenly the remaining 2 guards attack Manan from the back. Manan dodged it easily. He noticed that they both also have daggers. " That's cheating, I can't fight with you bare-handed. I think it's time to call up my weapons," Manan said humorously. He touches his hips and closes his eyes. He starts to breathe heavily. After a few seconds, he pulled up his hand and got 2 long katanas formed from light coming from his palm. " I think it will be too much for you," Manan said and then his one katana caught fire and turned into dust. " Now, I can finally be at your level by giving you an extra weapon," . Guards are constantly trying to attack Manan but they can not match the speed of Manan.

Manan's katana also blows with that red fire coming from his body, granting him immense speed. He hits their daggers one by one with a fast speed. He's so fast that guards can't match his speed. His attack obliterated their daggers. He hit guards with punches and knocked them down with a single blow.

"Such weaklings, you deserve painful deaths but I will make it easier because I am a nice guy after all," Manan said, " You cannot handle this! This is just 1% of the techniques and abilities I have learned. I repeat myself, don't you dare to touch my descendent," . By completing his words, he draws the sword and spells something " Crimson rose," . His Katana's flames took the shape of many butterflies and left the Katana. He draws his Katana and kills all 3 of them by cutting their heads. " Come on, give me something powerful, Mr. descendent," Manan smiles. His body turns to normal. He falls to the ground. Sehel wakes him up and notices that the cult has left the woods but without Rakshas' fluid. Manan stood up and went towards the bottle but then he heard someone running. Manan was very tired so he could not catch someone.

A guy in a denim jacket and trousers, a red hat, and a face half-covered with a piece of cloth came from behind and grabbed the bottle before Manan. Manan ordered Sehel " Sehel, go after him at full speed and grab him! I am coming slowly"

Chapter 7
Across the ages

Sehel runs at full speed but starts to lose energy. " That guy is so fast I don't think I can catch him but I have to," Said Sehel in his mind. He saw that guy opening the bottle of fluid. " Manan, come faster," Said Sehel loudly.

After some time, he heard someone running fast. It was Manan. Sehel stopped and took a sigh of relief. " Finally you are here," Sehel said and started to run again but slowly. Now Manan is chasing that guy. By running, they both reach the wall of the hostel. Suddenly, Manan falls to the ground and faints. That guy entered the hostel by jumping off the wall. Sehel approaches Manan. " Wake up Manan, He has entered the hostel," Said Sehel " Holy shit, we missed it," . There was an emotion in his voice for the first time that was tension. Somehow, he manages to enter the hostel with the body of Manan. He takes Manan to their room and throws him on the bed. He starts to clean up all the blood from his body. He splashes some water on his face. Manan got consciousness with ease. " Hey, Manan! That guy is in the hostel among us," said Sehel. Manan is perplexed " You know what Sehel, I had a dream when I fainted," Manan said " I saw a man with an ancient dress. He saw me and smiled brightly. His face was full of scars. After some time, I noticed that I couldn't move or speak anything. He patted my head and said ' Good job and Good luck Mr. Descendent' I have no idea what he said. He starts to say something ' Whenever you feel helpless or on the brink of death, I will come to rescue you. Finally, you formed a connection between us.' and you know what the worst part is, usually I can't remember my dreams but I can recall this word for word. He was also wearing a locket with a symbol and that symbol represents my bloodline. I don't know how but I was able to swap my body with that man and I think he was the strongest man in the Vidyvansh bloodline. So, is this my inherited powers just like you have, to swap my body with him,"

"What the hell you have just said makes kind of sense," Sehel said. They both forgot about that guy who was in the hostel. Manan gets up from the bed and closes his eyes. He starts to focus. " Oh man, what the hell is that, a massive steel chain? Is that thing called connection?," He sees all those things in his mind. He saw an old rusty steel chain with the label 'CONNECTION'. " Yes, this is our connection and I am impressed that you have mastered your mind at such a young age," that man is again here " Hey Manan, I am your ancestor Veerendra Indrajit Vidyavansh. " What is this chain?" Manan asks. Veerendra replies peacefully " That's just a visual representation of the connection you formed with me yesterday. You did a great job Manan and tension not, we cannot swap bodies without your permission" . Manan is standing confused and decides to return. He opens his eyes and tells everything to Sahel. Sehel listened to everything and got confused and said " A chain?" . Manan made a confused face and replied " Yes, a chain. It was very rusty and dirty. One label is stuck on it which says

'CONNECTION'" . Sehel said, " Umm.. interesting," . Manan grabs his journal and writes the heading *'CONNECTION'*. He starts to write everything down.

***

Almost 1 week has passed, summer holidays have started. Manan and Sehel are completing their sleep. They have almost forgotten about the guy in Hostel. Manan's sleep broke by hearing a knock on the door. He opens the door. One man is standing there " Letter for you," . He handed the letter to Manan and moved forward. Manan opens the seal of the letter and starts to read. The letter goes like this:

Dear Manan,

I heard that your holidays have started. If you don't mind, you can come to my house for this holiday. I have so many things to tell you and if you want, you can bring one of your friends with you.

I will come to pick you up tomorrow so be ready.

Sandeep

"Oh, he remembers me," Manan said. His voice is successful in waking Sehel up. Manan said, " Pack your bag, we are going to Sandeep's house," . Sehel got confused " Sandeep? Who is he?" His voice was a bit sleepy. Manan explains everything.

"My stomach is aching. let's go to refuel it," Manan said to Sehel. They slam the door and go to mess. After getting food on a plate, they start to search for a place where they can eat. Manan vision falls on a seat next to Advik. He waves Advik but Advik ignores it. Manan's hand falls. When they sit on the seat suddenly Advik stands up and goes to other places. " Eat your food, I am just coming," Manan said and left. He starts to follow Advik. He is in such a hurry that he doesn't notice one girl and bumps into her which results in the fall of her plate full of food. " I am sorry, I didn't see-" Manan saw her carefully and said " Devika?" . Devika smiles and replies " Hey, Manan?" . Manan said, " Yeah, What are you doing?" . " Fine, why did you leave without a reply that day?" Devika replies. Manan blushes " Actually, I was dumb that time," . " Don't say that. Ummm... My reply to that question will be yes" . Manan blushes very hard and smiles. Devika is about to go but Manan interferes. " Hey, can we go on a walk this evening?" Devika makes a cute face and her red cheeks squeeze a bit. " Sure, meet me on the big playground, "

Chapter 8
Departure

"Cool," Said Sehel " So you have made her go on a walk with you in the playground," . Manan sitting on his chair said " Yes, it will be interesting" Manan blushed. Sehel said, " You are forgetting something," . Manan gets tensed and remembers " Holy shit, Advik" We are going now to his room," . Sehel said " Not now, it's afternoon," . Manan replies " I will be with Devika in the evening, tomorrow we are going to Sandeep's house, Now is the best time to do something," . Sehel thinks and said " Fine, let's go then,"

Manan gets up from his table and Sehel from bed. Their legs start to run and Sehel's hands slam the door very hard. They rush to Advik's room. " But what will we ask him?" Sehel asked while running. " Why is he avoiding us? We will ask him that question only. I consider him suspicious," Manan replied.

They reach his room and knock on the door. There was no answer. Manan turned his head to check the lock but there was no lock. There is just a shiny but a bit rusty door latch which is open. Sehel pushes the door and surprisingly the door slides and opens.

Manan's eyes catch the whole scenario of the room. There is a bed with a messy bed sheet forming a big ball. There is a cupboard with 2 metallic handles. " I can sense something, I don't know what but I have felt it before a long time," Sehel said with a confused face. " What?" asked Manan. As Manan can interview about Sehel's condition, he hears someone in a haste" Hey, what are you doing here," . It was Advik. Advik is very scared and breathing laboriously. " Oh, hi, Advik," Manan hesitates. Sehel said, " Why the hell are you dodging us?" . Sehel said with no hesitancy and no shame. Manan was kind of impressed. Advik replied in anger " What if I ask you what are you doing in my room? Get out of here now you both!" . Manan, sitting on the bed, stood up and said " Mind your tongue, Advik. I can tolerate anything at any point but self-respect is like my jewellery and if somebody tries to clutch it, I overlook my boundaries." . Manan and Sehel leave the room. Manan grabs the handle of the door and hits the door of Advik's room. As soon as the door slammed, Tears from Advik's eyes drifted out without control. “ I am sorry for both of you. I swear it will help you both in the end,” Advik said in a crying voice.

***

Manan is sitting at his desk, reading a novel by J.K Rowling. Without seeing the clock, He is very busy reading and thinking of his confrontation with Advik. He suddenly remembers his evening walk with Devika. He gets up and grabs his T-shirt. “ I am going, Sehel,” Manan said. Manan notices Seal’s face “ Feeling jealous,” Manan smiles “ till I come back, read that demonic book. You will get a little knowledge,” Manan slams the door and goes to the playground. He is feeling nervous and excited also. As he walked through the hallway, His stomach got filled with butterflies. He reaches the playground and sees Devika. She is wearing a light blue coloured hoodie and narrow jeans. Additionally, she has opened hair which melts Manan’s heart. Manan is stunned for a moment. “ Hi?” Devika said in a confused and low-volume voice. Manan gets normal again. “ Oh hi, You look pretty,” Manan said. Devika lowers her head and smiles “ Thank you, Manan, You are also looking handsome,” . Manan blushes. They start to walk.

After a bit of normal conversation, they reached the Park bench. Devika sat there, and Manan also followed the lead. “ You know after our first interaction, Advik came to me and also wants to be a friend,” Devika said. “ Oh really, what was your reply to him?” Manan said. Devika replies “ I just said OK, But I didn’t expect that he would be such a good friend,” . Manan made an Impressive face “ So he is your friend. You know he is my friend too,” Manan looked down at his knees “ But I don’t know why he has been acting weird for the past few days,” .

Devika made a confused face. “ He is interacting well with me,” . There is a complete and awkward silence between them. Manan saw a guy in the playground. That guy waves Devika. Devika also replied with a handwave. He gets busy playing football. “ If you don’t mind, who is that guy?” Manan asks. “ Oh, He is my friend Ruhan,” Devika replied, “ I met him in class. I found him very funny and charming but still I consider him not more than a good friend,” . Manan took a sigh of relief. “ I think it right time, Manan, I accept you as you are. The thing I want to tell is that I....I Love You,” Devika said nervously. Manan is stunned again but he is surprised and excited. Manan stands up and makes eye contact with her. “ Me too,” Manan said and left. Manan is feeling very happy because Devika confessed before him. Manan enters the room and starts to jump in excitement. He starts to scream and shout. “ Man, What is happening to you?” said Sehel sitting on the chair reading that book. Manan turns his head to Sehel. “ Sehel, she confessed before me," . Sehel replied casually " I didn't see anything to celebrate," . Manan smiles " Oh come on," .

"Ah, yes, you got a letter from your Sandeep," Sehel said. Manan makes a confused face. " What? And you, give him some respect come on," . Manan takes the letter from the table.

'Dear Manan,

Sorry for the instant change in plan but pack your bags today only I am going to pick you up by night. I am just very excited to tell you something and 1 more thing, your friend should know about all paranormal shit or don't bring him.

Sandeep'

"Well, pack your bag today only, we are going to his house tonight,t," Said Manan " He can be at any time," . After tier conversation, they hear a horn outside of their window. It was Sandeep. " What? Now?" Manan screams from the window. " Yes, don't argue with me, just sit in my car," . Manan zips up his bag with many essentials like his journals. He hangs his bag on his shoulder. Sehel does the same. he picks up the lock and locks their room. They climb down the stairs and tell the receptionist about them.

Manan opens his car's door and throws himself and his bag. Sehel does the same.

Chapter 9
Hidden pursuit

"Are you here? lord Rakshas," Said a very deep voice coming from the forest. A human-sized white figure with a pure black face with only 2 small white flames, looking like eyes. The face was burning in a pure black fire. He said slowly pointing to the hostel. " I am coming for you my lord and if anyone tries to stop me, that will be their last mistake," .

That figure appears as a man's body. He lacks a nose, lips and ears. He just has that burning eyes full of desire without any pupils.

He runs away after hearing the snores of watchmen. Suddenly, Advik wakes up from his sleep in the shadows of a bright moon. He is breathing hard and rapidly. he seems to be very scared like he had experienced a nightmare. " Oh my god, what a scary dream! I think I should sleep, it's midnight." Advik said very slowly. He often does that, talking to himself.

He wakes up in the morning, free of any tension from school. His eyes are feeling very heavy and his body is craving for more sleep but he knows that sleeping at this moment will be a waste of time. So, he gets up and follows his morning routine. After all that, he goes to the bathroom and turns on the shower. The water is very cold. Advik can feel his muscles being active as splashes of cold water drain them. After some time, as he walks to the mess he meets Devika. He waves to her. She waves her back and calls her by hand sign. Advik walks to her and offers a handshake. She accepted and Advik felt the softness of her skin.

"Hey, it's been a long time since we talked," Advik said cheerfully, leaving her hand gently. She pulls her hand to her " Yeah, last time when we talked, I remember, you had to go to a football match." Devika said. Advik looked down and smiles.

Devika said out of the blue " Hey, I heard from Manan that you have been acting weird for the past few days. What happened?" Devika puts her hand on Advik's shoulder " You can tell me. trust me,"

"If you are worthy of my trust then come to my room I want to show you something," Advik said " Let's go," . Adviik and Devika leave the mess and walk to Advik's room. " So, I think Manan didn't tell you about this before but something exists in this world superior to humans," Advik said. Devika listens carefully. " And they are way more powerful than us. I only found Manan capable of defeating all of them because his abilities are so much different and powerful," . Devika looks at Advik with a confused face, " Whatever you just said, I didn't get anything," .

"Oh damn, see something exists in this world that is more powerful than us and they are mysteriously becoming active this year since Manan joined the school, and according to my theory, this is because of their curse that they can only be active for only 3 years in 1000 years and the first year has started." . Devika scratches her head " But Manan seems a bit normal, I don't think that he is engaged in this stuff," Devika said " If he pretends to be normal than I must say that he is a damn good actor," . Advik slams his hand to his forehead " You think this is a joke or something,"

"No, not at all. I believe everything you just said," Devika said smiling " I am a bit confused about it, I understand all of your theories but my question is how do you know about all of this,"

"I have nothing to hide now," Advik said downing his head.

"Devika, I trust you more than anyone now, I am—" Advik said. " The reincarnation of Karan," .

"Who is Karan? Who are you? I can't understand anything," Devika said in a shocking voice.

"Don't be sad. Karan, a fighter for peace, was a loyal and kind friend of Manan's father and Sandeep. I think you don't know about Sandeep. A few months back I got a letter from Manan's father revealing that he would come to his place. Karan was very excited as he would meet his friend after so long time. Arjun came to my house. Karan stood up and opened the door. Arjun was holding a vegetable knife. The knife was sharp and shiny. his eyes were full of tears. He said to go and take care of my son in the orphanage." Advik said " He put his hand on Karan's left ear and tilted his head. Arjun stabs the knife in Karan's neck. Karan can only remember finding himself in Advik's body," . The situation got tense. Devika swallows her saliva. " So, are you Karan or Advik?"

"I am both. I control Advik's body to protect Manan." Advik said " The real Advik is inactive for a while. That time I remember when Rakta was fighting with Manan in Advik's body and then also tried to control Rakta when Manan was unconscious. If I didn't stop Rakta that time, probably your love story wouldn't even start" .

"This is way too confusing, but I believe it," Devika said.

Chapter 10
Invade-1

Advik and Devika discussed that fight with Manan, sitting on the bed. After Advik completes a sentence, Devika raises a genuine question. Devika has all the knowledge about the paranormal world as their conversation ends.

"So you are saying that Manan is possessed by Rakta," Devika said.

"Yes, but here is a disadvantage of this possession," Advik said like a professor explaining a complex theory " If he has to switch his soul with Rakta, he will have to consume Agnivesh blood. Normal human blood will not tempt Rakta. Rakts only loves Agnivesh's blood. That's why he could not switch his souls in the woods" .

"What woods?" Devika asked.

"Recently, they went to approach a cult in the forest. Manan fought with 2 guards and tried to unleash Rakta but didn't know that he needed my blood to unleash him." Advik said.

"Damn! it is getting more confusing,"

Advik suddenly sighs opens his cupboard and shows Devika something. A red swirling, shiny liquid is kept in a glass bottle.

"Is that?" Devika asked with a shocked face

"Rakshas fluid. I am the one who stole the bottle from them," Advik said softly.

"Manan told me about that fluid a bit and I think that's why you were acting weird with them," Devika said " Right?" .

Advik nodes " I just want Manan in a safe place and Sandeep's house is the safest place for him and Sehel. Everything is according to my plan. I expect that today, the leader of the cult will come to take their lord back,"

"Today," Devika got terrified " but how are we gonna be able to defeat that leader,"

"We don't have to," Advik said smiling " You just have to follow my plan,"

***

Advik opened up his cupboard and picked up a big long box apart from the bottle. The wooden box is hefty with a shiny lock. Advik opens that lock. He lifts the lid of that box. The box contains a shiny, sharp and long axe with a wooden handle. The handle has a red and golden thread design with two pearls hanging with two red threads at the end of the handle

"Long time no see," Advik said smiling " Best gift I received from Sandeep" .

He picks up the axe and holds the handle tightly.

"Manan, let me do today's work. Your future is going to be harder," Advik said to himself. After a while, Advik sits alone in his room thinking about that leader.

Out of the blue, the weather changes and black clouds surround the hostel like a blanket. Suddenly, Advik hears an explosion sound from the woods. It is a thunderstrike. Some of the trees caught fire. Advik looks outside from his window. He noticed a human body figure in which his head was caught in black fire.

"He is here, oh my god," Advik said.

Students were sent outside the hostel for safety. The figure reveals himself, emerging from the fire with 2 eye-shaped glowing things on his face and the whole face is on fire. His body is purely white. He has a bulky, muscular look.

"Lord, are you here?" that figure roared in an intense, spine-chilling voice.

Then he noticed an axe thrown at him. He dodges it. The Axe strikes the ground and gets stuck. Out of the blue, Advik reaches the ground, holding the axe's handle.

"So, you are that cult leader," Advik said " You look a lot different from others" .

"give me lord Rakshas back," the leader said in a cold voice.

"And what if I said no?"

"You all will face the darkness of dark flames,"

"Dark flames, interesting," Advik said.

"Give me Lord Rakshas and I will cause just a bit of destruction," Leader said.

"That's cheating,"

Advik runs towards the leader and tries to hit him with an axe. When he drew the axe the leader was gone.

Chapter 11
Invade-2

Advik is shocked. his grip on his axe loosens and he feels coldness in the air. He can sense sorrowness and coldness in the environment. He notices a whiteness in the area and blackness in the sky. His eyes cannot believe what's happening to him. All of a sudden, he gets hit by a strong punch on his face.

The punch was so strong that it broke a bunch of Advik's bones in his jaw. He came back to his senses and realised the pain in the jaw.

"I told you, bastard. Give me my lord back, you still have time," said the white figure in a serious, heavy and cold voice.

Advik stands, grabs his jaw and shakes it. " Fight me for your lord,"

"Say it straight, you just want to die, right," said the leader.

His cold voice is enough to spread a coldness in the environment. Advik tightened his grip and said " For your knowledge, I have Agnivesh blood. That means I have Brunswick bloom flames,"

"Oh I see, The flames of the hidden garden, this type of flames can be only used by Agnivesh's blood," the leader said.

"I have wasted my 1 whole day yielding this power," Advik said in an angry voice. His body starts to burn in bright green flames. The flames are creating an aura of air rounding. The dust particle gets disturbed and starts to float in the air. " I am feeling way more powerful now,"

Advik's axe got covered in green flames. His axe is feeling more sharper. Out of the blue, advice swings his axe to the leader's neck. His axe got more swift and sharp because of his flames.

"Finally," Advik said.

His axe hits his neck but can't cut. His axe got cracks. The cracks started to get big and resulted in the shattering of the axe's blade into a thousand pieces.

Advik was shocked and became hopeless.

“Now this battle will be fair,” the leader said. “ No weapons. Just Brunswick flames vs dark flames,” . His voice becomes cold and deep with every word of his sentence.

Advik’s flames get smaller. His face became small. All the expressions leave his face. With a dull face, he starts to tremble. His only weapon just got shattered.

He doesn’t notice the leader standing behind him. A black structure bound Advik’s feet. The structure is looking like branches covered with black paint.

Advik tries to pull out his feet from branches but the branches are bonded too tightly that Advik can’t even move his feet. His breath starts to get faster.

“I have the power, right and will to kill you right now, brat. But I just want my lord back not your filthy life,” Leader said.

“Wh- what are that shit on my feet?” Advik said in a terrifying voice.

“I can make any structure through my dark flames.” The leader said in a laughing voice “ I didn’t expect to end Brunswick flame user this way,”

Leader lifts his pure white hand against Advik. A giant pointed structure emerged from the ground. The structure, breaking all the ground, shoots at Advik.

A sudden adrenaline rush flows into his body, granting him all the powers of Brunswick flames. The green flames got bigger and bigger and surrounded terrified Advik. Advik got teleported at the back.

“This is getting interesting now,” Leader said.

Advik kicks the leader on his back which pushes him back. His kick is burning like it is kept on a stove of green flames.

His flames are burning so much like petrol is poured into it. His eyes start to brighten, showing a sense of hope. The leader turns to Advik.

“I am feeling more dominant here,” Advik said and gave a smile with big bright eyes.

Advik starts to run fast towards the leader and punches his face. He was so fast that Leader can’t dodge it. The punch was so hard that the Leader’s head got shaken. His eyes were covered with blackness for a couple of seconds.

Advik taking advantage of these seconds, kicks his head again. The leader flew up and fell on the ground very hard.

Advik feels confident but then he notices he can't move.

He feels his hands and legs bound by black matter coming from the ground like a plant.

The leader gets up and laughs " Nice joke, I am always dominant in the field," the leader says coldly " Just plucking 1 leaf from the tree does not mean you can hack the tree, fool"

"You don't know me and Brunswick flames," Advik said in a struggling voice.

The black matter starts to get tight and begins to squeeze Advik's hands and legs.

Advik's face begins to get clenched and reddish. His eyes got enlarged in size. He inhales a lot of air and screams very loudly.

His flames are not on his body anymore but on the the whole ground. His eyes become red and black matter starts to break.

His hand and legs got free. The black matter started to disappear. Advik's power level at that time is more than the leader's. But Advik's mouth and nose begin to bleed.

"I am at my limits." Advik said, " I didn't expect Brunswick flames to be that powerful," .

Leader giggles " You are a tough opponent. Congratulations, you have got a compliment from me, Yaksha 24," he said, " Oh, did I just reveal my identity? Does it matter?" .

Advik, in a beast-like condition, listens to all the information Yaksh just told. But now, he can't hear anything anymore.

Chapter 12
Bluff

Blood trickles from his ears, and a piercing pain shoots through his head. Advik realizes he's gone deaf. The pain intensifies, and he clutches his ears, screaming silently into the void.

He has lost all his hope of winning. The green flames start to vanish. He turned normal again, panting. His eyes, ears and mouth are bleeding very much. His vision got blurry. He can't hear anything. He falls to his knees and looks down. His blood got mixed with tears in his eyes.

"Such a fool, you have more power than me but still," Yaksh said " You defeated yourself. I didn't even reach my potential fighting to you,"

Yaksh lifts his hand and puts it on Advik's head; mysteriously, his ears start to heal and all blood disappears. Slowly, he can hear everything now.

"But why?" Advik said getting up.

"Your prize, Advik," Yaksh said.

His hearing sense was recovered by Yaksh.

"Now give me fluid, I don't want to create more chaos here," Yaksh said.

"What will happen if I gave fluid to him? The fluid is an awakening of the strongest soulbound till now. I have to get rid of him temporarily," Advik thinks.

"I said give me the fluid," Yaksha said. He forms a gigantic needle-like structure pointed just an inch away from Advik's right eye. Advik breath stops for a moment. " Fine, I will give that fluid," Advik said " but on one condition,"

"What condition?" Yaksh said.

"You have to leave this place without giving a scratch to anyone," Advik said in a serious tone.

"I agree," said Yaksha.

Advik puts his hand on the back pocket of his pants. He withdraws a tiny glass bottle filled with Rakshas fluid.

"That's all I have," Advik throws that bottle, expecting Yaksha to catch.

"We will meet soon," said Yaksha.

Yaksha got covered in a cloud of black smoke. He vanished along with smoke.

Suddenly, Advik fell to the ground. His eyes closed slowly. His body becomes as light as a feather.

A leaf, floating in the air fell on his back.

***

Advik stays in that condition for 2 days. He got to his senses in a mid-afternoon. He saw Devika sitting next to him, reading a newspaper.

"Hi," Advik said in a woolly voice.

Devika's eyes began to come out. Her mouth opened up.

"Finally, you are at your senses" .

"why am I here?" Advik said.

"When police enter the hostel. They found nothing but you lying down with closed eyes." Devika said, " You saved all of us from that monster, Advik" .

"No," Advik said in a low voice " He will surely return when he will find out that the fluid I have given is not Rakshas fluid but Rakta fluid,"

"What?" Devika said " So, why did you fight with him if ultimately you have to give him Rakta fluid,"

"Now, he will think that if I had fought so hard then it must be Rakshas fluid I am carrying," Advik said " So, he took it without even checking,"

"You are smarter than I think," Devika said.

Advik smiles softly. " Devika, I want you to write a letter to Sandeep informing them all about this incident," Advik said " I can't write it because of my injured arms and I also have some personal reasons,"

"OK, I will write to him right now." DevikaC goes to her room and grabs paper, a clipboard and a pen. She rushes to the medical area where Advik is being treated.

***

“Wake up, Manan,” Sandeep said, shaking Manan’s leg “ It’s already 6:00 AM. We are already 2 hours late for the mission,”

Manan, lying in bed, wakes up. “ What mission?” Manan’s wooly voice echoes in Sandeep’s ear.

“Seems like you forget. We are training to be powerful and get control over our flames” .

“Oh please, don’t remind me of flames,” Manan said, rubbing his eyes “ Can you please explain clearly what are flames?”

“That’s our only mission, actually I even don’t know much about it but I do know that you have used it during your fight with the cult,” Sandeep said in a deep voice.

“And what is the mission?” Manan asked.

“I strongly believe that your dad has discovered it and jotted it down in one of the journals,” Sandeep said.

“But I have all of my father’s journals,” Manan said.

“Not all,” Sandeep said. “ I think this will not ring the bell”

“What do you mean?” Manan asked.

“Arjun told me something about drawer 2,” Sandeep said, “ He said that drawer 2 contains accurate information about flames of the inner being” .

“What?” Manan said in a loud voice “ Oh yes drawer 2, I remember now” .

“I will wait outside and bring Sehel also, he seems interesting,” Sandeep said.

Manan and Sehel reach a massive gate of Sandeep’s house. They saw Sandeep lying on the bonnet.

“Get in the car now, kids”

Chapter 13
Emergency

Manan and Sehel reach a massive gate of Sandeep's house. They saw Sandeep lying on the bonnet.

He starts his car and rides to Manan's house. Manan and Sehel open the car door and place their feet in front of Manan's house. The house's gate, made up of iron, is like a jail cell.

"Let's get inside," Manan said. He opens the gate. Sandeep and Sehel followed him. They enter the main hall with stairs going down to the basement. The house is looking like the spider's web generator. It is covered with dust and spider webs. They approach the basement. Manan notices that letter written by his dad.

Manan picked up the letter and kept it in his pocket. Sandeep tried hard to open that drawer. His big muscle of arms tightens up. At the next moment, the entire desk shatters and the drawer is opened. The pieces of wood spread across the floor.

"Sorry about the desk, Manan," Sandeep said smiling.

"Doesn't matter," said Manan lowering his head " Not anymore,"

Sandeep redeems a journal from that drawer. The journal is very thin. It hardly contains 4 pages.

Sandeep opens the journal's 1st page and starts to read.

FLAMES

God wants to create human most powerful human being in existence. So He gave dark flames in humans. But humans are the most evil thing. Through these Dark flames, humans created 3 soulbounds. God realizes that it is getting worse.

So he limited flames to only 2 bloodlines. 1 of the first members of a bloodline creates Brunswick flames and one creates Crimson flames. Brunswick flames are considered to be the most powerful flames out of 3 of them. The weakest flames are crimson flames. But limiting flames in 2 bloodlines is not enough. Humans start to learn all kinds of flames regardless of their bloodlines.

That was a history of flames (According to me, this can be wrong). Most of the normal human has dark flames in it but tkey don't know how to use them. Then Vidyavansh's blood (my blood) wields crimson flames. Then tke supreme blood of Agnivesh blood wields the most powerful flames of all time.

Now different flame users can create various techniques for themselves. One example of this technique is black veins. This technique infuses crimson flames in blood flowing in limbs and gives the veins a black colour. It temporarily increases the physical abilities of the individual. It also neutralises allthe attacks of Soulbounds.

Now here are some ofthemost elite attacks on flame users

1. Flentity summon

This attack lets the user to summon a beast to help in a battle. These beasts aremadeby consistent visualisation by users.

2. Sky manipulation

This attack lets the user manipulate the nature of the sky and infuse some attacks in it. Only crimson flames and dark flames users are capable of doing this.

The main generator of the flames is the sky's atmosphere. After using this attack, the user's bones were disabled for 10 minutes. So this attack is considered as the final attack of the user.

"Your father was bad at writing," Sandeep said after reading " He had a poor choice of words. Hardly anyone can understand,"

"But I like the concept of flames," Manan said, " Sandeep, according to this you and Sehel are dark flame users, right?"

"Yeah," Sandeep said, " But I think we have to contact anyone who knows everything about flame" .

"I know someone who can help us," Manan said.

After a few moments, " Why is he taking so long?" Sandeep asked by looking at Manan sitting with closed eyes.

"He is talking to someone," Sehel said " He will be back at senses in a short time,"

Manan finds himself talking to Veerendra in front of the massive chain with the tag 'CONNECTION'.

"So you are saying that Sandeep and Sehel have more potential than me," Manan said.

"Yes, but you are still more powerful than all of your allies," Said a manly voice of Veerendra " Flames are just a weapon, one must know how to use it to be strong" .

"And what are sky manipulation and Flentity summon?" Manan asked.

"These are the elite moves of the legendary flame wielder," Veerendra said, " I can use these moves along with 5 different attacks I have created with crimson flames" .

"I just want to know one thing now," Manan said " Why are you trapped in my body,"

"Curse," Veerandra said " It's a long story I will tell you in brief My father was the strongest dark flame user of his time. He was powerful but selfish and obsessed with his blood. My brother, Ashwith Indrajit Agnivesh, was also following my father's ideology. But I was different and I prioritise humanity more than bloodline. When I got married and blessed with a boy, Rakshas attacked the village. Father ordered me to go and bring Rakshas's head to him. I am not that much strong at that time. So I was defeated by him. That was the only time I have begged someone. I can communicate with him by using flame transfer. He proposed a deal that if I gave him my son, he would leave the village and I said OK,"

"But why,?" Manan asked.

"So that village will be safe," Veerandra said " My father cursed me that I will not let any of my descendants get killed by Soulbounds or flames. So, I just came to help every descendent,"

"Thanks for all of the information you have provided," Manan said.

He gets back to his senses. He is breathing heavily.

"Not much lead," Manan said " Let's go home,"

They all head towards the car and open the doors. Sandeep drives to his home.

Manan keeps his hand on the car handle door and opens it. Sandeep notices 1 letter kept in front of the main door. The letter was 1 day late.

Sandeep reads the letter and checks the date. Immediately he rushes to the car and calls Sehel and Manan.

"Emergency," Sandeep said, " Sit in the car" .

Chapter 14
Unchain

"You made the biggest mistake of your life," Yaksha said looking at Advik.

"What are these chains? I can't use flames," Advik said struggling. He is tired in front of a tree in the woods. Yaksha is standing in front of him with his hand fully covered with dark flames.

"Chain force," Yaksha said " One of my skills I have created with dark flames. It stops the flow of flames in the victim" .

"I promise I will give you that fluid," Advik said struggling " I am feeling thirsty,"

"Let me end all of your struggle," Yaksha said in a cold voice, " I will find fluid by myself" .

Yaksha points his hand covered in dark flames towards Advik's face. Advik got trembled. One Dark solid needle-shaped structure emerges from the ground and shoots towards Advik's face.

Advik is about to die with that structure but one big thing rushes and smashes the structure and breaks it. Advik rotates his head and sees a car. Sandeep, Sehel and Manan open the car's door. Manan's eyes filled with anger. His face became expressionless. He is casually walking towards Yaksha. Yaksha rotated his head and took a glance at Manan.

"So much flames you possess, little kid," Yaksha said

"Watch out, Manan, he is Yaksha," Sandeep said.

"How you dare to touch him!" Manan screams. Manan took a stance and punched Yaksha in his face. He doesn't move a bit.

"Get away kid," Yaksha said, hitting Manan with his punch so fast that Manan couldn't dodge it. Manan flew through the air and fell to the ground.

"Watch out Manan," Advik Said loudly " He is stronger than you think,"

Sandeep and Sehel rush to Manan.

"Manan, he is Yaksha," Sandeep said " He is a strong dark flames user,"

"I'll handle Yaksha. Get Advik free, now!"

Manan gets up and runs towards Yaksha fast, landing a very powerful punch on his face. Yaksha flew and fell to the ground.

"What? How Manan How?" Sandeep said in shock.

"You will get used to it," Sehel said " How are we supposed to break those chains,"

"I have a way," Sandeep said.

They both rush for advice but a wall of black substance forms before them.

"You both think I will let you there so easily," Yaksha said.

Advik's hands are tightly bound with chains, stopping blood flow. His thirst for water takes over and his eyes get blacked out. A black screen appears in front of him.

"Save me, Sandeep," Advik said slowly.

3 more walls emerged across Sandeep and Sehel. The walls have caged them.

"Oh man, this shitty man is pissing me off," Sandeep said in an angry voice.

"You are pretty fast kid," Yaksha said, getting up.

Manan rushes towards Advik to unchain him. Suddenly notices that his legs and hands are tied with black substance.

"Let me over it," Yaksha said. One needle-pointed structure emerges from the ground and is about to stab Manan.

Manan smiles for a millisecond and vanishes.

"Don't you dare touch him," Manan said in a manly voice.

"Who is that?" Sandeep asks Sehel in a cage.

"Veerendra," Sehel said " he is here,"

Manan sitting on a piece of rock said " Show me what you got, Ugly bitch,"

Manan stood up and put his hand on his hip. He got bright and 2 long Katana forms from light. The Katanas got covered with crimson flames.

"Who are you?" Yaksha said, " You are not that boy" .

"I am your worst nightmare," Manan said smiling.

Manan rushes and jumps very high. He landed on Yaksha with his sword stabbed into his heart. Yaksha falls.

"You are not dead as I expected, It will be hard to reach to your heart," . One wall made up of a black structure separates them.

Manan punches the wall and the wall is shattered into many small pieces.

"Oh, Man," Sandeep said, This cage is pissing me off,"

He punches to one point in the cage and the whole cage vanishes.

"Wow," Sehel said, " How did you do that?"

"Nullify punch," Sandeep said, " One of my skills, it is not time to analyse my power Let unchain that boy" .

Yaksha is in a weak state so he cannot stop them. Sandeep and Sehel go to Advik who has merely fainted. Sandeep punches the chain and it vanishes.

Advik fell on his knee and faints. Sandeep is about to stand and get him some water from the car, but he notices that his legs are bound with those chains. Sehel also got bounded by a chain. Their hands and legs are bound.

"Foolish humans," Yaksha said laughing " You can never break those chains," . Suddenly Yaksha feels a punch on his face.

"Fight me," Manan said.

Manan again punched but Yaksha held it and crumbled his fist.

His fists got covered with crimson flames. He punches Yaksa with his other hand.

Yaksha kicks Manan and he flies and falls to the ground. Manan limbs got paralyzed.

"Why can't I move them?" Veerendra said in Manan's body.

"Paralysis kick," Yaksha said, " I have more power than creating those structures" .

Then a black structure, shaped as brick emerges from the ground and shoots at Manan's face. Manan got lying down on the tree.

He is panting heavily.

"You are a good competition but still," Yaksha said.

"I am sorry Manan." Veerendra said " I don't know if I can return,"

"Let me over this" .

Again, a needle-shaped structure emerged.

Manan smiles " I am preparing,"

"For what," Yaksha said.

Manan raised his blood-covered smiling face.

"Sky manipulation: Eternal blackhole," Manan screams in a manly voice.

Suddenly the sky turns to a bright red colour and the atmosphere gets filled with anger and tension.

Chapter 15
" It can't be him"

"This attack will heal Manan and also take 80% of Yaksha's flames," Veerendra thought, focusing his energy. " Give it your best, Mr. Descendent" .

Manan regained consciousness, his eyes widening at the massive black hole forming in the scarlet sky.

"What is this?" Sandeep asked, still bound. He looked at Advik, whose eyes were slowly opening.

"What's happening?" Manan murmured, disoriented.

Yaksha stood at the centre of the field, just below the black hole. It sucked up his flames, draining 80% of his power. Manan saw an opening. He sprinted towards Yaksha and punched him in the face, feeling his skin softening. Yaksha staggered back, panting.

Sandeep, now free from the chains, delivered another punch to Yaksha. " His flames are gone," Sandeep realized.

Yaksha tried to run but saw an axe before him. Advik stood in his path. " We have an unresolved issue," Advik said coldly.

"I broke that axe," Yaksha said, wincing in pain.

"Weapon reinforcement," Advik replied, his eyes steely. " You're not the only one with techniques" .

Advik took a stance, ready to strike. But Yaksha darted towards Manan, only to stop mysteriously.

"I am proud of you all," Yaksha said loudly. " Especially you, Manan. The world you see now is not the one you will experience in the future" .

"What?" Manan asked, his voice filled with shock. " Who are you?"

But it was too late. Advik's axe, covered in Brunswick flames, sliced Yaksha's head clean off. His body disintegrated into dust, blown away by the wind.

Manan's mind raced with questions, overthinking consuming him. The realization hit him hard. " No! No!" Manan cried, falling to his knees. " It can't be him!"

"Manan!" Advik shouted, placing a hand on his shoulder. " What happened?"

Manan's screams and cries echoed, resonating with everyone.

Manan after a moment faints down.

***

1 DAY LATER

"Oh, so the saviour one is awake," Sandeep said to Manan who is lying on hospital bed with two drips of glucose.

Sandeep shows him a newspaper. The newspaper is showing a whole article about that incident in the woods. The article states:

After the incident in the woods of a small village, Khander proves the existence of some powers more than we know. This incident gives more content to research on for the researcher.

"Ok That's enough," Sandeep said grabbing the newspaper.

"Where are the others?" Manan asks.

"At my place," Sandeep said " You are the one left for treatment,"

"One last thing," Manan said, " Who is Yaksha exactly?"

"I don't know," Sandeep said, " I got this from your jacket's pocket If you have permission so can I open it?"

"Yeah you can," Manan said.

Sandeep opens the letter from Manan's father. He notices something different.

"Manan," Saneep said " Are you sure this is written by your father,"

"Yes"

"Then, it's a problem," Sandeep said " The journal I read and this letter's handwriting is completely different,"

"What?" Manan said.

"Yes," Sandeep said " Your father was kidnapped or something by someone stronger than us,"

"What?" Manan said " We should gather more information. Let's go to your place. We will find the one who kidnapped my father and I will give him or her most brutal death,"

Darkness has spread worldwide but some crimson light is making some space in it.

GLOSSERY

Welcome to the glossary for our epic tale, a thrilling journey filled with action, mystery, and deep character connections. This glossary is designed to help you navigate the intricate world of Manan, Advik, and their companions as they face formidable adversaries and uncover shocking truths. Here, you'll find detailed explanations of the characters, their unique abilities, key terms, and significant locations that shape the narrative. Whether you're revisiting the story or exploring it for the first time, this glossary will serve as your guide to understanding the complex and captivating elements that make up this adventure. Dive in and relive the excitement as you explore the heart and soul of this epic saga.

In this story, the characters, abilities, and locations create a rich and immersive world. At the heart of the narrative is **Manan**, the protagonist, who possesses extraordinary flame abilities. His journey drives the narrative forward, culminating in the dramatic revelation that Yaksha, the primary antagonist, is connected to his father. Manan's powers is to sap body with Veerendra which powers include the ability to summon katanas enveloped in crimson flames, making him a formidable force in battles.

Advik, a key ally, begins the story in a dire situation, chained and unable to use his latent flame abilities. His rescue by friends like **Sandeep** and **Sehel** sets the stage for his crucial role in the story's climax, where he decapitates Yaksha in a surprising twist. Advik's journey from powerlessness to pivotal action highlights his importance in the narrative.

Sandeep stands out as a strong character, known for his physical prowers and unique skill, the " Nullify Punch, " which can break any structure or cage. His reliability and strength are crucial in saving Advik and supporting his allies during intense battles. **Sehel**, though initially without powers, provides vital support and plays a significant role in the group's efforts against their enemies.

Yaksha, the main antagonist, wields dark flame abilities that make him a formidable opponent. His skills include **Chain Force**, which halts the flow of flames in his victims, rendering them powerless. Yaksha's dark flames can also create solid structures and paralysis attacks, adding layers to his menacing presence. The revelation of his identity as Manan's father adds depth and complexity to his character.

Veerendra demonstrates his power with the ultimate attack, **Eternal Blackhole**, which creates a black hole in the sky, absorbing a substantial portion of Yaksha's flames. This attack showcases the high stakes and intense power struggles within the story. Veerendra's actions significantly impact the narrative, especially during the critical moments of the climax.

The story's power system revolves around the concept of **flames**, used by various characters to enhance their combat abilities. These flames are central to the battles and conflicts that define the narrative. **Paralysis Kick**, another ability used by Yaksha, paralyzes opponents, rendering them immobile and adding to the tension of the confrontations.

The **woods** serve as a significant location in the story, where Advik is initially chained, and a major battle against Yaksha unfolds. This setting provides a backdrop for critical events, including the dramatic rescue of Advik and the intense confrontations with Yaksha. The **tree** in the woods is a focal point where pivotal battles occur, leading to the climax of the story.

Throughout the narrative, the **fluid** remains a mysterious element that Advik promises to give Yaksha, indicating its importance in the story's power dynamics. This fluid adds an element of intrigue and mystery, contributing to the story's overall depth.

This glossary offers a comprehensive guide to understanding the characters, abilities, and key elements that define this epic narrative. It enhances the reading experience by providing deeper insights into the intricate world of the story.